9/06

$15.99

j
CAR

Carris, Joan Davenport
    Welcome to the Bed &
Biscuit

Joan Carris

illustrated by Noah Z. Jones

CANDLEWICK PRESS
CAMBRIDGE, MASSACHUSETTS

J
CAR

Text copyright © 2006 by Joan Carris
Illustrations copyright © 2006 by Noah Z. Jones

First edition 2006

Library of Congress Cataloging-in-Publication Data
Carris, Joan Davenport.
Welcome to the Bed and Biscuit / Joan Carris ; illustrated by Noah Jones
p.   cm.
Summary: The family animals at the Bed and Biscuit begin to feel slighted
when Dr. Bender returns from a fire with something that occupies
the time usually reserved for them.
ISBN-13: 978-0-7636-2151-3
ISBN-10: 0-7636-2151-X
[1. Veterinarians — Fiction. 2. Animals — Fiction. 3. Fire extinction — Fiction.]
I. Jones, Noah (Noah Z.) ill.
PZ7.C2347We 2006
[Fic] — dc22   2004062857

2 4 6 8 10 9 7 5 3 1

Printed in the United States of America

This book was typeset in Ole Claude.
The illustrations were done in pencil and watercolor.

Candlewick Press
2067 Massachusetts Avenue
Cambridge, Massachusetts 02140

visit us at www.candlewick.com

For Marguerite Murray, Phyllis Reynolds Naylor,
and Peggy Thomson — my writers' group —
who first listened to this story
and cheered me on
J. C.

For my mom and dad
N. J.

Contents

1
Welcome

"WELCOME TO THE BED AND BISCUIT!" The large multicolored bird sat on the desk, holding the phone receiver up to her orange beak with one claw.

"Hand it here, Gabby," said Grampa Bender, seated at the desk. He wore a slender, red-gold cat curled around his neck like a scarf.

"Right now." Grampa pried the receiver out of Gabby's claw.

" 'Morning," he said into the phone. "Dr. Adam Bender here. Sorry for the delay. How may I help you?"

He listened a bit, then said, "Yes, ma'am, mynah birds *are* amazing. Gabby sounds just like me . . . or anything else she wants to copy.

Now, about your dog, Frou-Frou. I have space to board her. You say she's a Pekingese?"

On the floor by his feet, the mini-pig Ernest listened briefly, then closed his eyes. *Silly things, Pekingese dogs.* Ernest had no time for them.

Grampa hung up the phone, but it rang again right away. Gabby grabbed it as before and again had to give it up.

Grampa listened, then said, "You mean today? Five goats?"

Ernest perked up. More boarders were coming, and that meant a busy day. As Grampa's main helper, he would be needed, which always made him feel good. In Ernest's opinion, everyone should have a pet pig.

Grampa hung up the phone. "Next time I get to answer it first," he told Gabby. "Now, why don't you count the pencils?"

The cat stretched out her neck and yawned, showing tiny, sharp teeth. She blinked sleepily, resettled herself around Grampa's neck, and began licking his ear. Lick . . . lick . . . lick.

Grampa petted her. "Milly, it's clean now, okay?"

Milly went right on licking.

He put down his pen and unwrapped the cat from his neck. "I sure hope you have kittens when you grow up. Then you'll have somebody else to clean."

He rubbed noses with his cat. "You keep Ernest company," he said, setting her on the floor beside the pig. "I need to—well, phooey! There goes the phone again. Didn't know I was so popular.

"Bed and Biscuit. Dr. Bender." He was quiet briefly, then laughed out loud. "No problem! You can bring Sherlock anytime. He's one of our favorites. See you later."

Ernest agreed with Grampa. Sherlock was an interesting old bluetick hound. He told fine stories.

As Grampa finished working, Gabby stuck the last pencils in the mug and began singing. "Happy BIRTH-day, dear ERN-est, Happy

BIRTH-day to yeww-OOO!" Ruffling her deep purple and green feathers, she leaned over the desk to look down at the pig.

Ernest gazed up at her. "You remembered," he said. "I'm three years old today. A fair age for a pig."

Grampa grinned at his noisy pets. "I give up," he said. "Nobody wants to be inside, so let's get out of here." Again wearing Milly like a scarf, he left the office. Gabby rode on Ernest's head, her favorite seat on the pig, and they went toward the dog kennels.

At the kennel doorway, Milly jumped lightly to the ground. Dogs were often scary, and much too loud. She streaked off toward the pastures. Grampa got busy measuring out feed for the dogs. Ernest carried pails of water in his strong jaws. Grampa cleaned cages and whistled. "Keeps my mind off the manure," he had told Ernest when Ernest was just a piglet.

Gabby whistled with him. Today they were doing "You Ain't Nothin' but a Hound Dog" in memory of Elvis Presley.

Ernest dragged each boarder's bedding outside, shook it vigorously, then replaced it. The dogs barked and yipped until Grampa brushed each one. It took a couple of hours, as five of the eight dog stalls had boarders.

When the goats arrived, Grampa and Ernest herded them into the closest pasture. Next, Mrs. Farringforth brought Frou-Frou the Pekingese to board for two weeks, and immediately after that came Sherlock, the bluetick hound. Sherlock ambled out into the grassy run attached to his indoor kennel.

"Glad to have you back," Ernest told the hound. "I'll stop by later, but we're busy right now."

Next to Sherlock, Frou-Frou was hurling herself at the wire fencing around her run. "Yip-yip! Yip-yip! Yip-yip!"

Sherlock eyed her mournfully before turning to Ernest. "Yappy little dust mop, and right next door. Just my luck."

"As soon as a boarder goes," Ernest said as he was leaving, "I'll move Frou-Frou's bedding over to that cage."

In the large far pastures, Ernest helped Grampa to feed and water the big animals—his horse, Beauty; the four cows; Romeo the donkey; and a small herd of llamas. That done, they stopped in the small pasture next to the house so that Grampa could check the health of the five new goats.

At last, Grampa and Ernest went to the house for lunch. On the porch—in the center of the mat, where no one could miss it—lay a dead mouse. Milly rested smugly on the porch swing.

"Good kitty!" Grampa picked up the mouse. "Haven't had a mouse in the house since I got you."

Before going in, Ernest rinsed off in his own personal pig shower. Grampa had built it for him beside the porch. One pull on the chain and

water cascaded all over Ernest. Today he treated himself to an extra-long birthday shower.

Grampa stuck his head out the door. "That'll do, Ernest."

Ernest tugged on the chain reluctantly. He liked to stand on his sparkly white stones under the lovely water for a long, long time.

A huge crow landed beside him with a rude "Caw!" A second crow . . . and a third. The first crow snatched one of the shiniest stones from Ernest's shower and flew off with it in his beak. Another stabbed his black beak right between Ernest's front hooves.

Ernest squealed in fury as the crow trio winged away, toward the woods behind the house and barn. His loud oinking carried across the grounds of the Bed and Biscuit. Every animal heard Ernest yelling at the thieving crows.

So did Grampa. "Ernest!" he called out the door. "Time to come in!"

* * *

After lunch Grampa set a golden cake in front of Ernest. "It's corn bread, just for you, because you have been my best buddy for three years. I don't know what I did without you, Ernest. Happy birthday."

Ernest had been all upset about the crows. Now he remembered why he was the luckiest pig in the world.

Looking up at Grampa, Ernest thought, *I wish he understood animal talk. I need to say thank you.*

"Would I like it?" Milly asked, hovering over the corn-bread cake.

"No," said Ernest, taking a big mouthful.

His pleasure in the cake was interrupted by a fire engine siren, followed by the ringing phone. Snout in the air, Ernest detected a faint smell of smoke.

Grampa lifted the phone receiver and listened. "Be right there," was all he said. He lifted Gabby off the back of a chair and put her on Ernest's blanket pile, next to Milly.

"Listen up, troops," he said, patting Ernest's head. "You three stay here! There's a fire over at McBroom's farm, and we can't let it spread to the woods between us. I'll be back after we put the fire out. You just *stay right here!*"

He grabbed a faded red cap, yanked open the door, and was gone.

Be very careful! Ernest longed to say in a way Grampa would understand. *We're your family and we worry. I can take care of everything here.*

"I'm scared," Milly murmured, gluing herself to Ernest's left haunch.

"Don't be such a baby!" snapped Gabby. She turned to Ernest. "Why can't that man just stay home? Why does he always have to go help people?"

"Because that's who he is," Ernest replied.

Milly pawed the blankets and kneaded Ernest awhile before settling against him. "Thank you for sharing your bed," she said.

"You're welcome." *Sort of,* he thought. Not only had his birthday party been cut short, but now he had both the cat and the bird *in bed with him.* A nap with Milly now and then was okay, but he preferred sleeping alone.

Ernest stretched out, his snout pointed at the door. Smoke and fire were bad. They always meant trouble.

2
The Mystery Box

HOURS WENT BY as the animals slept, and night came.

"You're snoring! Snoring!" Gabby poked Ernest with her beak.

"Sorry," Ernest said, half asleep. She went back to sleep, but he was now wide awake, worrying.

"Ernest! You're squishing me!" Milly cried.

How could such a small cat take over the whole bed? Ernest apologized again, and the night wore on. Above the old black stove, the clock ticked away.

Grampa's rooster, Rory — the loudest rooster in the county — began crowing as dawn approached. Ernest clung to the hope that someday Rory would be made into chicken soup. He had chased Ernest repeatedly when he was a piglet, new to the Bed and Biscuit.

Now Ernest stuck his head under a blanket and lay still. Finally Grampa's white pickup truck roared by the kitchen window. Ernest, Milly, and Gabby lined up at the low window to watch.

Grampa hurried into the barn and came out with a dark wooden box — about the size of a breadbox. He entered the kitchen with a tired,

"'Morning, troops," and went on by, heading for the stairs to his bedroom.

They listened as he slowly mounted the steps.

"Well, wouldn't that frost your beak!" Gabby said from her perch on the back of a chair.

"Oh, hush," Ernest said.

Gabby stuck her beak in the air. "Ah, Lord Ernest Piglet is at it again." She turned her back and talked to the wall. "I'll never know why Grampa had to add a bossy pig to this family."

"You won't figure it out, either, birdbrain!"

Gabby whirled around. "Blabby little fat-belly!"

"Sorry excuse for a parrot!"

"Porky smart-mouth!"

Ernest was running out of insults. What was Grampa doing anyway?

"Loudmouth lard-bucket!"

Milly gave a pitiful mew.

Eager to change the subject, Ernest said, "You win. So what do we think Grampa got out of the barn? I never saw that box before."

"He had something in his arms, too, when he got out of the truck," Milly said. "It's a bundle. I saw it."

"Really?" said Ernest. "Did he have it when he came through here?"

Milly's ears flattened and she shook out her fur. "I don't know, but I'm going up there to see for myself. It's my bedroom, too!"

"Well, wouldn't that frost your beak!" Gabby said.

Time passed. Ernest fidgeted.

Gabby flew from the rocking chair to the end of the kitchen counter and began to clean her shimmering purple-green tailfeathers.

"Do you think the bundle came from McBroom's farm?" Ernest asked her.

"Who knows? Grampa was gone all night. He could have been all over the county."

"Well, how about that box? Do you know what it's for?"

"Honestly! Can't you see I'm busy?"

"But this is important!"

Gabby stopped preening. "How do you know?"

"I just do."

At that point Milly marched into the kitchen. She sat on Ernest's bed where the white tip of her striped tail tapped up and down. *Tap . . . tap . . . tap.*

Ernest said, "Well? What is Grampa doing? Tell us about the box."

"It's hot," she said. "I felt it with my whiskers when I tried to look inside."

"Is it a toaster?" Ernest asked. "Is Grampa cooking in his room?"

"No, but it plugs into the wall like a toaster."

Suddenly Gabby cried, "The bundle! Tell us about the bundle!"

Milly's green eyes narrowed. "The bundle is

in the box. I tried to get a look at it, and Grampa pushed me away." Her tail tapped faster.

"You poor thing," Gabby said with unusual sympathy.

"Now, Milly, Grampa's just tired," said Ernest. "He thinks you're the best cat in the world."

Milly drooped. "Right now, all he cares about is what's *in that box.*"

Ernest went on. "Maybe whatever is in the box could hurt you, Milly."

"Right. Most likely a pit bull," Gabby said.

Unamused, Ernest and Milly stared at her.

"Just trying to lighten things up!" Gabby said, waggling her beak.

"Seriously," Milly went on, "how could it hurt me? It's tiny!"

"You're sure the bundle is inside the box? And it isn't food?"

"I'm sure. He's talking to it." Milly glared at Gabby and Ernest. "Have you ever seen Grampa talk to his lunch?"

"No, but he talks to the newspaper and the TV . . . and of course, he always talks to us." Ernest stopped short.

"There," said Milly.

Ernest bent down and nuzzled her satiny head. "You think what's in the box is alive, don't you?"

"Yes. And it stinks."

"Stinks?" Ernest and Gabby said together.

"Like the barbecue grill. Outside, where we have picnics."

"Hmm." Ernest was thoughtful. "So it smells like smoke."

"Yes," Milly said. "It smells burned, too. But Grampa must think it's wonderful. He hardly even noticed I was in the room. So I left."

Ernest saw how upset she was. She had slept with Grampa ever since he had found her hiding, tiny and terrified, in his barn. She was so sickly that he had fed her with an eyedropper and carried her around in his jacket pocket. He called her his Milly-Baby, and from the beginning, his bed had been her bed.

"I'm not going back up there," Milly announced. "I'll just sleep with you, Ernest— like I did last night—if that's all right?"

"Oh . . . fine . . . sure," Ernest lied gallantly.

"I'm on the curtain rod, Milly, in case you need me," said Gabby.

But who, or what, was upstairs with Grampa? Ernest wondered.

3

Smaller Than a Breadbox

ONLY A COUPLE OF HOURS LATER, a sleepy-eyed Grampa left for morning milking. Now that it was eight o'clock, the cows were bawling constantly.

Milly sat up on Ernest's bed. "He left me behind!"

"Me, too," Ernest replied. "He's tired, that's all. I'm going to the barn to help. Those milk pails are heavy. You coming?"

"Absolutely not," Milly said.

"No pouting," Gabby said from under the kitchen table, where she was hunting for crumbs. "Only babies pout."

"But I *am* a baby," Milly said.

Ernest bumped the old door to make it open. He decided not to remind Milly that she was nearly a year old — almost full grown.

Out on the porch, Ernest cast a professional eye over the property. Ahead of him stretched the large, grassy square between their house and the red brick office. On the left side of the square was the low white building of dog kennels, with a matching building for cats on the right. Once Ernest had spied an escaped cat boarder there, crouching on the lower limb of a maple tree. His warning oinks had alerted

Grampa, who came and retrieved the cat. Ever since, Ernest had scouted the property several times a day.

Inspection over, Ernest trotted off to his right, down the dirt lane to the barn, some distance behind their house. As usual he helped Grampa carry heavy things like pails of milk and water, and he listened when Grampa talked to him. Grampa needed listeners, because Gramma Bender had died just before Ernest came, and Grampa was still lonely.

With the cows milked and the chickens fed, Ernest and Grampa went back to the house. Grampa talked some more while he made breakfast.

"Cows have no flexibility," he told his family. "They think the world is ending if they aren't milked before seven in the morning and by six in the evening."

Ernest munched hungrily on his stew of potatoes, eggs, bread, and fresh milk. He needed to keep up his strength. With several new boarders and the problem in the breadbox upstairs, it could be a difficult day.

Swallowing the last tasty crust of bread, Ernest moseyed over to his bed, where he could think. What was small enough to fit in a breadbox?

Across the room, Grampa enjoyed a second mug of coffee. By the time he set his dishes in the sink, he was whistling.

"I'm off to the kennels," Grampa said. He stroked Milly's sleek back, but she did not turn around to lick his hand this time. She didn't roll over to have her belly rubbed either.

Ernest stood at the window and watched Grampa walk away. "He left us behind again," Ernest said.

"Tailfeathers!" cried Gabby. "The man is not himself. He gave me two pears for breakfast, not one."

"Well, I ate nothing, and he didn't even notice," said Milly. "He's thinking only of that thing in the box."

"You mean the baby," Gabby said.

"*Baby!* Who said it was a baby?" squawled Milly.

"No one, but it probably *is*," Ernest explained. "That box must be like the heated chick brooder in the barn for those fool chicken babies."

"Of course," Gabby agreed. "It could be any kind of baby at all—a mouse, a wild bird ... you know Grampa!"

Milly's eyes glittered. "We don't need another baby in the family!"

"'Baby in the family,'" Gabby repeated.

Ernest shot Gabby a warning look. He was in no mood for her mynah-bird repeats. "Not *in our family*," he told Milly. "Grampa's a vet, remember? We take care of animals here all the time."

"Not in our bedroom!"

"True," said Ernest, "but we think this one was in the fire. Maybe it's in pain, and that's why he pushed you away."

Milly's tail had become a quivering bottle brush. "But it's in OUR bedroom! Looks like family to me!"

"Well, I'm going out there to help Grampa, just like always."

Milly hunkered down stubbornly on the bed of blankets, but Gabby hopped onto Ernest's head.

"Take me to the office," she ordered. "I have work to do."

"What do you mean? Are you answering the office phone again?"

"When Grampa's away I run the office," Gabby said.

Stunned, Ernest repeated, "You *run the office*?"

"Why not? I can sound just like Grampa. And that ringing phone is hard on my nerves!"

Ernest knew she could make any sound she wanted. Her imitation of a garbage truck backing up was his favorite. But now he said, "Gabby, you know you shouldn't be answering that phone!"

Gabby flapped one wing, dismissing the advice.

"Is it fun to talk on the phone?" Milly asked.

"Oh, yes! I say, 'Welcome to the Bed and Biscuit,' and people say, 'How's life treating you, Dr. Bender?'"

"Um, what do you say then?" asked Ernest, alarmed.

"Oh, it varies," she replied. "Sometimes I say life is treating me like a bowl of fruit."

"How creative!" said Milly.

Gabby nodded happily. "Other times I say life is treating me like a dead pigeon. It all depends on my mood."

"Oh, dear, dear," Ernest mumbled. "Gabby," he went on, "do you take calls from people who want to board their pets?"

"Of course," she said, ruffling her feathers importantly.

Milly quivered with awe. "This is so impressive, Gabby!"

Ernest kept on. "Do you take *reservations* for boarding?"

"Why should I tell *you*?"

"Because this is Grampa's business, not some game with a phone!"

"Oooh!" squawked Gabby. "Mr. Self-Important Pig again! Picking on a poor senior-citizen bird!"

Ernest waited. He said nothing.

"Oh, all right," Gabby admitted. "Usually I say we're full. 'Call back tomorrow,' I tell them."

Ernest said, "Well, then, that's fine."

"Sometimes I say, 'Toodle-OO to you!' at the end."

Of course Grampa would *never* say that. "Anything else?" Ernest asked.

Gabby broke into a noisy cackle. "Yesterday I did make a joke, but only on one call."

"Go on," Ernest said, steeling himself.

"I think it's very original," she began. "I said, 'Hello, Comfort Inn. But we're all out of comfort!'" She cackled proudly.

Milly gave a small, sad mew. "You reminded me," she said. "'All out of comfort.' That's just how I feel."

Ernest fumed with anger. *It's a wonder we get any business at all if Gabby talks like that on the phone,* he thought.

"Gabby," he said firmly, "let the answering machine in the office take those phone calls. That's its job!"

"Arrk! You mean I'm being replaced by a machine?"

"'Being replaced,'" echoed Milly with another mournful mew.

4

A Gift of Moles

TWO DAYS WENT BY. Grampa ran from the office to the house and back again. Ernest followed him upstairs once, even though he loathed steps, like all pigs. He wanted to see exactly what was going on.

Grampa was feeding the tiny bundle, talking to it, holding it against his chest. He even hummed to it now and then.

A baby for sure, thought Ernest, turning away. *And still in Grampa's room. Here in our house.* But Ernest told no one what he'd seen. Instead, he tried to pretend that nothing had changed.

During this time, Milly sat on Ernest's bed and watched Grampa come and go without her. The autumn days were growing cooler, but apparently he no longer needed his living cat scarf.

After supper on the second day, Milly scooted out the pet door. She did not return until almost bedtime. Then, wet and bedraggled, with a dead mole clutched in her teeth, she pushed her way through the pet door. Inside, she laid the mole on the mat in front of the little door. She went back out, returning with another mole, which she arranged beside the first.

"Good job!" Ernest said. "Grampa hates moles in the yard. And you got a double-header!"

"Thank you," Milly said. "It's what cats do for their humans. And *only cats do this,* as far as I know."

"Right! I don't know any pigs who catch mice and moles for their humans."

At bedtime Grampa appeared briefly in the kitchen. Just long enough to say, " 'Night, troops. See you in the morning. Come on, Milly, bedtime!" He snapped off the light and was gone.

Ernest heard Milly's disappointed mew. *"Now, Milly,"* he said, "Grampa had no chance to even see those moles. Just wait till morning. And he *did* call you to come to bed, you know. *Just like last night."*

Milly sat like a statue. She didn't even blink.

The next morning was the third one after the fire, and it started fast. The phone rang twice before Grampa could even get downstairs. By then the cows were bawling again.

"Dang telephones," Grampa said, dashing into the kitchen. "My grandparents lived on this farm and did fine without them. If you needed to ask somebody's advice, you rode over there on your horse. It was friendlier and the folks always fed you something good."

By this time he was in his jacket, with his red cap on his head. He jerked open the heavy door and clattered down the porch steps. The big old door simply brushed aside Milly's moles that lay on the mat.

"Now, Milly," Ernest began, but it was no good. Milly had seen everything. Those were full-grown moles, and Ernest knew she had fought hard for them. They were special gifts, and they had been overlooked.

Milly crept over to the pet door, picked up a mole, and pushed open the door.

"Bad kitty!" Gabby squawked after her. "You put that back where Grampa can find it!"

Gabby kept on squawking. Milly ignored her as she returned, then left with the second mole. This time she stayed outside.

"Well, wouldn't that frost—"

"Oh, put a sock in it," Ernest said. "I'm going to talk to Sherlock."

Gabby's voice shrilled after him. "Bad pig! Bad pig!"

At the kennels Ernest flopped down on the other side of the fence from the sleeping bluetick hound. *Guess I'll wait till he wakes up,* Ernest thought.

Sherlock's large, round nose twitched, then snuffled. He opened one eye. "Smelled you," he said. "Cleanest pig I ever met."

"Of course. I have my own shower. Give any pig a shower, and he'll be just as clean as I am."

Sherlock rippled his skin, stretched, and sat up inch by inch. "So why do pigs roll in mud?"

"To keep the hot sun from burning us up. If we overheat, we die. Mud keeps us cool. Of course, a shower is better."

"I hate baths. Did I tell you about my last coon hunt?"

Ernest shook his head no, which was a lie. He had heard this particular story many times, about how Sherlock had treed six coons all by himself in one night. But Ernest would listen again to be polite. It was important to keep the boarders happy. Grampa often said that.

After lunch that day, Grampa did not just doze in his rocking chair. He took off his glasses and lay down on the couch in the family room, next to the kitchen.

Gabby flew in to check and came back to the kitchen. "Snoring," she said. "Out like a light."

"Of course," came a small voice. "He's up at night fussing with that baby."

"Awwk!" went Gabby. "Where are you?"

"She's behind the stove," Ernest said.

Now Milly oozed out from behind the wood stove, an enormous, black stove that had been in Grampa's family forever. It sat in the same place, angled in the corner where air could circulate around it. No one cleaned behind it, because only bugs or a small animal could get back there.

"Milly," Ernest said, "any day now, things will be back to normal around here. We just have to be patient."

Milly sniffed. "Until then I'll be behind the stove. It's a good place for thinking." She stood up and gave Ernest a lick on his head. Almost like a farewell lick.

She nodded at Gabby, who never permitted any licking from cats, and said, "I want to be alone. Nothing's the same anymore, and it makes me sad."

Milly was behind the stove again before Gabby or Ernest could reply.

5
Mad Milly

THE NEXT DAY AT BREAKFAST, Grampa called for Milly, but he was too busy to do more than call. When he left for the office, he set out food and water for her.

This was barn-cleaning day. Grampa called it "mucking out." As he finished mucking out a stall, Ernest nosed in piles of fresh straw. Ernest added a pail of fresh water, and they moved on to the next stall.

Grampa was not whistling. He always whistled when he was cleaning up stinky stuff, but not today. He went over to the house regularly, but he did not talk about it. That evening after supper, he put his head down on the table and began snoring.

Up on her curtain rod, Gabby sang, "Rock-a-bye, BAAY-BEEE, on the TREE-TOPPP!" Only an exhausted man could have slept through it.

Ernest settled on his blankets and ordered his brain to get busy on their problem. He had talked to his brain other times, with excellent results. The idea was to relax, to let the mind operate at its own speed. Trusting in this, he stretched out and promptly fell asleep.

After a short doze, Ernest woke up. Grampa was still at the table, but now he was talking to himself. "No use hunting for her. She's avoiding me on purpose. So *jealous* she can't see . . . and all cats *hate changes.* Dangit, she's apt to run off!"

Elbows on his knees, Grampa leaned over toward Ernest. "Have you seen Milly? I've looked everywhere. Her food's still there, too."

"Wrunk." Ernest went to rub against Grampa's leg.

"Go find her, Ernest. Please? *Find Milly.*"

Like most pigs, Ernest could find things that humans or other animals couldn't. Just last week his marvelous snout had found Grampa's missing wallet, under the seat in the pickup.

But right now Ernest knew Milly was hurt and hiding on purpose. Of course, Grampa was hurting, too.

Ernest made up his mind. He had a duty to the family. And so he posed like a pointer at the back corner of the wood stove. The hanging lamp over the stove gave just enough light to reveal a furry golden ball in the dark corner.

Gabby landed on Ernest's head and peered into the dimness. "Aack! Filthy!"

Her eyes big, Milly went, "Sssss!"

Grampa knelt on creaky knees and looked behind the stove. "Ah, you did it, Ernest!" He reached one hand in, toward his cat.

"Milly, girl, I sure miss you," he began. "Don't hide back there!"

No answer. Only silence in the kitchen.

Grampa kept coaxing, but Milly did not move, and finally he stood up. He put out fresh food and water, close to the stove corner.

He set Gabby on his finger, told her what a fine bird she was, and stroked her iridescent feathers. He patted Ernest for a long time.

"Poor Milly," he said at last. "I guess I'll leave her alone for now. She's just being a cat after all."

"Wrunk," said Ernest.

"But you're my pig, thank goodness, and we understand each other."

Grampa was slow getting to the kitchen the next morning. He'd had only a sip of coffee when the phone rang.

"'Morning!" he said. Then, "Oh, I'm fine, AnnaLee. Just too busy. If it gets any busier, I'll put you back on the payroll for after school, okay?

"How are your folks?" he went on. "I know it'll take a long time to get over your loss. Fire's a terrible thing."

Grampa listened quite awhile. "You're rebuilding *right there*? Well, hallelujah!"

"Hal-le-LU-jah! Hal-le-LU-jah!" crowed Gabby, savoring the new word.

Grampa continued, more serious now. "Well, AnnaLee, it's been five days, you know. He's still in the incubator. I've had a new idea, but I'm not promising a thing."

Hmm, Ernest thought. *Our mystery baby is a HE.* Ernest saw the flick of Milly's marmalade tail at the back corner of the stove.

"INC-u-ba-tor! INC-u-ba-tor!" Gabby sang.

When Grampa hung up the phone and left for milking, Ernest hurried over to the stove. "For corn's sake, Milly," he said, "come on out here! Grampa is miserable without you."

Ernest went on urging her to use her head — to think of Grampa — to remember how folks in a family helped one another. When Milly did not reply, he gave up and went outdoors.

Sherlock's lugubrious howl called him to the hound's pen.

Ernest jogged right over. "Hi. How's it going?"

"Awful slow," Sherlock said. "And that dust mop never shuts up. Whines all the time. Spoiled rotten."

Ernest had been trying to ignore the yipping Frou-Frou, but it was impossible. "Maybe she's bored, like you," he suggested. "What if you told her some of your exciting stories about

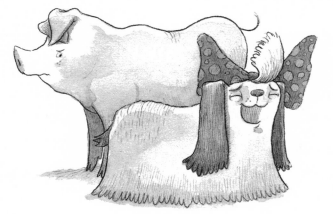

coon hunts? You could explain possum hunting, too. It would be a fine, educational way to pass the time."

Sherlock's eyebrows lifted. "Well . . . if you think . . ."

"Oh, I do!" Ernest assured him. "And you'd be doing Grampa—the whole place, really—a real service by keeping her quiet."

"Be more like a miracle," Sherlock observed. "But I'm happy to help out." He turned his attention to the Pekingese, and Ernest went on to the barn to help with milking.

After breakfast Grampa said, "Gabby, Ernest— stay right where you are. I've got something to show you." He loped toward the stairs and was soon back, standing in the kitchen doorway.

"Ta-da! What do you think? It was up in the attic—left over from our last child." Grampa was wearing a green flannel baby-snuggler.

"Very handy, see? I can sit down to feed him wherever I am. He'll hear my heartbeat and be warm, too."

Gabby flew to Grampa's shoulder. Ernest stood by Grampa's feet and let his snout go to work. *Mm-hmm,* he thought, *it's burned, all right.*

"Okay, troops, no touching, but you can have a peek." Grampa knelt so Ernest could see, and opened the flap on the green snuggler.

6

Poor Little Guy

QUIVERING WITH CURIOSITY, Ernest and Gabby gazed down into the baby-snuggler.

"It's a wee Scottie," whispered Grampa. "Like I had when I was a boy."

Ernest saw a black furry mite of a dog at the bottom of the snuggler. With its closed eyes and singed fur, it seemed more dead than alive.

This thing hasn't a chance, thought Ernest. *Grampa shouldn't get his hopes up.* Ernest sagged back onto his haunches.

Gabby examined the puppy and gave a puzzled "Awwwk?" She looked from Grampa to

Ernest and back at Grampa, her beak tilted to one side.

"I see you're not impressed," Grampa said. "But this is a miracle here! We don't know *how* his mother got him out of the barn the day of the fire!"

Grampa stood up. "And he won't make it unless he takes more formula. I sure wish his mama had lived to nurse him."

"Wrunk," Ernest said softly, wishing yet again that he and Grampa could talk. It was a pity humans had so little skill with languages.

Grampa took a tiny bottle out of the refrigerator and warmed it under hot running water. "Chow time, buddy." He settled into the kitchen's plaid overstuffed chair with the puppy.

Ernest glanced under the stove and watched Milly's thrashing tail.

The clock ticked and Grampa talked. "You're my wee Scotch laddie," he crooned to the puppy. "A braw wee laddie, for sure. And you're going to drink all this formula, aren't you?"

Hmm, Ernest thought. *He never called ME a braw wee laddie.*

Later that day, after chores were finished, Ernest trotted off to the barn alone. *I'm still waiting patiently,* he told his brain as he selected apples from a feed bin.

Gabby flew in and settled on the rim of the bin. "'Wee laddie, wee laddie,'" she mimicked. "It's sickening! If I hear it one more time, I'm moving to the woods with the crows."

Ernest stopped eating. *Gabby hates those crows,* he thought, *just like I do.* "You wouldn't do that, would you?"

"I might! This morning they took more of my shiny stones," she said. "My shiny picture stones! They're always taking something!"

"You mean those stones under my shower?"

"Those are *my picture stones.* I make beautiful designs with them. When I move to the woods, I'll find them and bring them back where they belong!"

Ernest said, "Those crows are tough. And huge. You be careful."

Gabby hopped to the barn floor and walked off, tailfeathers high. "Well, I'm tough too, so I just might go live with them. And I might not."

Ernest watched her leave as he crunched his last apple. *Now both Milly and Gabby are mad,* he thought. *And Grampa's grumpy because he's tired.*

Ernest went home for a shower. He stood under the soothing water a long time before

going inside to dry off on his blankets. First, though, he checked behind the stove for Milly.

"She's there," Grampa said from his chair by the window. "Poor little pussycat. I don't know where Gabby went. But look here, Ernest. Seems to me our laddie is perkier. He's taken more formula today."

The pup quivered a little and tried to melt into Grampa's chest — or so it seemed to Ernest — but he made no sound.

"Poor wee orphan," Grampa said. "Lost everything, didn't you? Right down to a few chimney bricks. But you're a miracle, laddie."

Jealousy ate into Ernest's heart. Now he knew exactly how Milly and Gabby felt. It was a mean feeling.

Of course, I was an orphan, too. He thought back to the day he had come to the Bed and Biscuit — tiny and cold and scared. His mother had died when he and his littermates were only a week old. He barely remembered her, only that she had fed him often and kept him toasty warm.

At the Bed and Biscuit, Grampa had also fed him often, wrapped him in blankets, and put him in a basket by the stove. *Then one day I went exploring,* Ernest recalled happily.

"Excuse me," Grampa said, moving his leg. "I have to fix a mug of tea."

Ernest hadn't realized he'd been leaning against Grampa's leg.

When Grampa had his tea, he sat down again. He patted his leg so that Ernest would sit beside him.

"Perhaps," Grampa said thoughtfully, "we should call him Lucky." He looked inside the snuggler and bent over so that Ernest could see.

The pup raised his head this time, but his eyes hadn't opened yet. His nose was dull, not shiny and healthy.

Grampa gazed fondly at the puppy. "I wish you'd make some kind of sound, fella. Any kind at all. Or did all that smoke ruin your bark? Maybe you're never going to bark for us, is that it?"

Ernest pressed against Grampa's leg. *That dog isn't even TRYING to bark,* Ernest thought. *His eyes aren't open, either.* Ernest recalled that Grampa had said the pup was a "preemie," born early.

All of a sudden Ernest thought, *Poor little guy. Of course Grampa wants to save him and give him a home. It's just the kind of thing he would do.*

And poor Grampa, because I don't think this orphan's going to make it.

7

Trying Days

GABBY BARGED INTO THE KITCHEN late that evening. The minute she saw Ernest, she started in.

"I'm *sick* of this!" she exclaimed. "Grampa has no time for *any* of us anymore, and it's *all that stinky Scottie's fault.* Well, I'm here, *too*! And I'm a *gorgeous, exotic bird* from *Vietnam*. I can talk *just like a human*! That ratty little dog says *nothing*. Now just *think about that*!"

"I'm thinking," Ernest said, backing away from her large, advancing beak.

"Loudmouth crows! I hate crows!" Gabby shrilled. She opened her beak wide and made a rude sound.

Ernest had a hunch that she would not move to the woods. After a bit he said, "I thought of something a while ago."

"It had better be good!"

"Well . . . I was thinking back to when I came here. Grampa wrapped me in a blanket and put me in a basket by the stove. He held me and fed me every few hours. AnnaLee McBroom fed me, too."

"Don't lecture me!"

"I was just remembering what happens with babies," he said mildly.

"I was a baby here, too! The *only* baby. Grampa was all mine for ten years! Then you came . . . and Milly . . . and now another one! Where will it end?" She gestured with one wing and nearly fell over.

Righting herself, Gabby said, "Where's Milly?"

Ernest inclined his head toward the stove.

Gabby gazed into the dark stove corner. "You know this is silly," she began.

Ernest interrupted quickly. "Milly is *thinking,* Gabby. We can count on her to use her head. Let's go to sleep now. It's late."

"Bossiest, most know-it-all pig I ever met," Gabby muttered. But she settled down on his blankets. In time, comforted by the place and by each other, they slept.

Two days crawled by. After supper on the eighth day after the fire, Grampa brought a tan willow basket down from the attic. He wrapped the puppy in a new red plaid blanket and tucked him into the basket near the stove.

"Keep an eye on him, Ernest," said Grampa. "I need a night's sleep with no interruptions. He should be fine there."

Grampa went to the back corner of the stove. "Can't see a blamed thing," he grumped. "Milly, if you're there, I still need you to be my kitty. I love you, you know." He snuffled noisily.

"And I sure hope nobody comes in while I'm talking to my stove. Blast it anyway!" He petted Ernest and Gabby, and practically ran upstairs to bed.

The puppy did not move, and he made no sound. Ernest watched him and thought, *You're in my basket. Well . . . not really,* he decided. *It's probably the new-baby basket for our whole family.*

He tried to remember if he had suffered like this puppy when he was new to the Bed and Biscuit. Well, no. He had just been lonely and scared.

"Were you sick like this dog when you came here?" he asked Gabby, who was on her curtain rod already, eyes closed.

"I have never been sick as a dog," she replied without opening her eyes.

"You know what I mean!"

"Okay, okay! This is all very sad. I agree. Now go to sleep."

Ernest nudged his blankets into nighttime position and gradually sank into a worried sleep.

The moon had risen high over the house when Ernest awoke with a snort. There, sitting right in front of him, licking her left paw, was Milly.

"Milly!" cried Ernest. He bounced up onto his haunches.

"About time!" Gabby flapped down from the curtain rod.

"Is that dog going to make it or not?" Milly asked.

Ernest hated hearing that question. "We hope so," he said firmly. "Being in that basket is progress. That was my basket when I was new here."

Milly slumped down on Ernest's bed. After a bit she said, "I'm mad at him, but Grampa is a very good human."

"Go to the head of the class!" snapped Gabby.

"No arguing," Ernest pleaded. "Isn't it nice that we're all here together? Just like old times. It's almost a party."

"A party with food?" Milly asked. "I'm hungry."

Ernest jumped to his hooves. With his snout he opened the refrigerator. "Just hop up there," he told Milly. "See that nice roast chicken?"

Milly leaped upward and balanced delicately on the refrigerator shelf. She gripped the carcass with her teeth and jumped down to the floor. "Oof," she said on landing. "This is a lot of chicken."

"If it's too much," Ernest said, "I can help."

"Get me a pear while you're in there," Gabby said.

Ernest snouted open the crisper and removed a pear for Gabby and one for himself. "Party time," he said joyfully.

The chicken and pears were soon eaten. Ernest put his hoof on the lever that raised the lid of the garbage can, and Gabby dropped in the chicken bones. Milly licked the floor clean. Grampa was a stickler about tidying up after meals.

After washing her face and paws, Milly crept around the puppy's basket. She moved in a crouch, ears flattened.

"Ssss," Milly said. Then "Fffftt!" in case the Scottie hadn't understood.

"Mill-eee!" Ernest warned.

Gabby tuned up. "You put your right wing IN. You put your right wing OUT. You put your right wing IN, and you shake it all about. You do—"

Milly glared at her. "What do you think you're doing?"

"Lightening things up. Ernest said we were having a party."

Ernest went over to Milly, who was much too close to the basket in his opinion. "Come on, Milly. A dog can never take the place of a cat! Go snuggle up to Grampa. He misses you—"

"Just look at that nice basket," Milly said. "And the special blanket. I didn't get anything like that when I came!"

"You were in Grampa's pocket!" Gabby said. "Next thing we knew, you were tearing all over the house. Giving us palpitations of the heart!"

True, Ernest thought, remembering. "Think about that!" he told Milly. "We didn't ask Grampa for a cat. But you came, and now we cannot imagine life without you! See how it works?"

Gabby squawked. "I never asked for a pig, either! Ten years here and I never needed a pig for one second!" She cackled noisily. "At least he doesn't snore very often."

"Don't break your beak complimenting me," said Ernest.

Slowly, Milly nodded. "Thank you. I'll think about it." And with that, she went back behind the stove.

"Oh, for corn's sake!" cried Ernest.

Gabby hummed softly, "You put your right wing in. . . ."

8

The Red Plaid Blanket

THE NEXT MORNING Grampa fixed everyone's breakfast, then sat down to feed the puppy. He was humming as usual when suddenly he yelped.

"Ernest! Gabby! Come here and look!"

Ernest stared at the pup's damp eye slits. *I guess his eyes are open,* Ernest thought, *but he's doing a lot of blinking. What a struggle he's having.*

From her perch on Ernest's head, Gabby went, "Oh, dear, dear."

"Okay," Grampa said firmly, "we have to give you a name. How about Sir William the Hardy? He was a great big, tough old Scot."

Ernest saw the puppy stop drinking. He gave Grampa a dark, silent look.

Grampa laughed out loud, something he hadn't done since the fire. "Got me there, didn't you? You little short Scottie, you!" Smiling broadly, he finished the feeding and wrapped the pup in his red plaid blanket.

"Oops, running late," Grampa said after a glance at the clock. He left the kitchen and headed toward his office.

"Let's go," Gabby said. "I belong in the office, too."

"Oh, please," Ernest said testily. "But I guess we might as well go. I need to be working. It helps me to think. We need to get back to where we were. Peaceful. Everyone getting along."

On their way out, Ernest stopped at the dog's basket. "You just hang in there," he said. "This is a good place."

The pup's tiny, squinched-up eyes stared vacantly ahead. Ernest wasn't sure the dog could see or hear. He didn't move and made no sound. He just lay there, wrapped in his Scotch plaid blanket.

Cleaning and feeding the dogs and cats filled much of the morning. Grampa had to shampoo the golden lab named Happy so he could go home. Happy jerked around and grumbled as the warm water soaked his thick, wavy fur.

Ernest stood by. "A bath is a beautiful thing," he told Happy. "I shower many times a day in hot weather. We pigs don't sweat, you know."

"If I'm hot, I go to a shady place," Happy said. "Baths are for humans."

"And pigs," Ernest insisted.

Soon Happy settled down, for which Grampa was thankful. He was sure Ernest had calmed the retriever. He knew that animals communicated in ways that only they understood.

Ernest watched Happy leave in his human's car, then immediately trotted over to Sherlock's outdoor run. "I can move Frou-Frou now — four stalls away," he told the hound.

"Who asked *you*?" demanded Frou-Frou.

Ernest looked over at her, then back at Sherlock.

"Aw . . . you don't have to go to all that trouble, Ernest," drawled the hound. "She'd . . . uh . . . she'd be —"

"All alone over there!" said Frou-Frou. "We'll call you if we need you. Goodbye, little pig."

Ernest decided that he didn't understand either Sherlock or Frou-Frou, and he didn't want to. He left, irritated at being called "little pig." *Of course,* he thought, *if I weren't a very small pig, I couldn't live in Grampa's house. There are worse things than being a little pig . . . such as being a dopey chicken.*

At noon Grampa, Gabby, and Ernest went back to the house for lunch.

"I'll bet our wee bairn is good and hungry by now," Grampa said, nodding at the puppy's basket. "Well, shoot! Where's the blanket?"

Grampa bent down, unbuttoned his flannel shirt, and tucked the puppy in against his chest. "I guess it's back to the snuggler for you.

"But where in heck is your blanket? It can't walk, and nobody's been here!" Grampa headed toward the stairs, in a hurry to get the snuggler.

"Bad kitty!" said Gabby. "Bad kitty!"

Ernest checked behind the stove. No Milly. Right away he inspected the kitchen. The family room. The small half-bath on the first floor. The dining room, seldom used since Gramma had died.

Ernest examined his blankets. Everything downstairs was as it should be except for the missing red blanket . . . and cat. Both gone at the same time.

Gabby fluttered down to sit in front of him. "Ernest, I have a million talents, but finding blankets is not one of them. It's up to you. Except for Grampa, you're the smartest one here."

Ernest was amazed. Gabby rarely complimented anyone.

Together they watched Grampa come into the kitchen. He wore the puppy in the snuggler and began fixing lunches, as always. Gazing into the refrigerator, he said, "Where's my chicken?"

"'My chicken!'" Gabby echoed.

Grampa moved things around in the refrigerator for some time before he gave up and set a package of bologna on the counter.

"I sure don't remember finishing that chicken." While he made himself a sandwich, Grampa groused about losing his mind. When he checked behind the stove for Milly and didn't see her, the look on his face darkened.

Slumped on his blankets, Ernest thought, *Drat that cat!* He hated to assume she had taken the blanket.

Still, he thought, *she could have, after the rest of us left for the office this morning. Maybe she thought that without his blanket, the puppy would get chilled . . . and sick . . . and then . . .* Ernest couldn't force himself to even think it.

And now she doesn't dare come back, he decided. *She'll hate herself for what she's done. She'll think she can never come home and be loved again. But that's not how families work. We understand. We just want her back!*

9

The Magnificent Snout

ERNEST BEGAN HUNTING for the blanket by taking a shower. A long shower always let him relax and think clearly. *Finding the blanket will be easy,* he concluded. *It will smell just like the puppy—like a smoky barbecue grill.*

Carefully he sniffed around the house's foundation. Through the beds of dried-up day lilies. Down the walk edged with purple asters.

Romeo's heehaw interrupted him. Ernest trotted over to the fence that separated the yard from the pasture. "Have you seen Milly?"

"I don't think so. Why?" Romeo's furry gray ears stood erect.

"She's missing. Have you seen anything *suspicious* today?"

"What's that mean?"

"A suspicious thing is *odd* in some way. For example, you might get a feeding when it isn't *time* for one. Or there's a *dog* on your doorstep when you expected a *cat*."

"I don't have a doorstep."

"Okay, okay! What I mean is, has anything *different* happened this morning? What did you see exactly?"

"Well . . . I saw the cows . . . Grampa's horse, Beauty . . . those noisy crows from the woods. Lots of mice. Will that do?"

Ernest gave up asking subtle questions and went straight to the point. "Romeo, did you see anything red? Did you see Milly dragging anything, maybe carrying something in her mouth?"

"You'd better tell me what the hay is going on!"

Ernest explained.

"Yup, a catastrophe. Get it? *Cat*astrophe?" brayed Romeo. "You folks need a *new cat.* Just tell me what kind — tiger stripe, black coat, alley cat, fancy longhair. I got connections. I can get any kind you want."

"Thank you, but Grampa wants his own cat back."

"That's a human for you!" Romeo heehawed.

"As humans go, Grampa is the pick of the litter!" Ernest turned and stomped off.

"Don't go away mad. Just go away!" Romeo nearly fell over heehawing.

Smart-aleck donkey, Ernest thought. *He gives me a pain in the brain.*

Still angry, Ernest entered the barn. It had always been Milly's favorite place, ever since Grampa had found her here. Also, she liked keeping the barn free of mice.

Ernest decided to ask the chickens first, though he had little hope of learning anything useful. "You folks seen anything odd today?" he began.

The chickens clucked among themselves. One scruffy white hen said, "What'll you give us if we tell you?"

"What do you want?"

"What have you got?"

"Well, nothing, really. I just thought —"

"How about crushed corn?" the scruffy hen said, her head tilted. She aimed one bright, hard eye at Ernest.

"I guess I could get some. Then you'll talk. Is it a deal?"

"Deal, pig. Get the corn."

Ernest backed away. "Just watch where you're pointing that beak," he said. He marched in a most dignified way to the feed room. Using his snout, he scooped crushed corn into an old pie pan. *I can't believe I'm bribing a chicken,* he thought gloomily. *A chicken.*

He set the corn in front of the chickens and said, "Okay, talk."

The white hen said, "Well, this morning Lolita gave an extra quart. That is *very odd*." She bent down to peck corn with the rest of the small flock.

"That's it?" he squealed. "You think that's special?"

"Can *you* give milk?" The hen had the sense to fly to the top board of a nearby stall. Safe there, she said, "Any other questions, small pig?"

Filled with fury, Ernest turned away. Chickens drove him crazy.

He moved on, inspecting each stall for traces of Milly. He smelled the tack room, the feed room, and the manure pile out back, even though it hurt his nose.

He went back inside the barn and crunched an apple to help himself feel better. *I was counting on her being here,* Ernest thought. He saw the ladder to the loft, but that was hopeless. *No pig has ever gone up to a barn loft,* he told himself, *and I'm not going to be the first.*

Carrying on with the search, Ernest poked his snout here and there for the entire length of the woodpile and the blooming thickets of purple hearts. Gramma's overgrown flower beds made perfect hiding places.

He pushed aside some yellow chrysanthemums behind the tall stone grill. *Yessir,* he thought, *this grill has the right smell.*

He stopped short. His brain had finally given him an idea. *How clever!* he thought. *How sneaky! I have to see what's inside that grill.*

With extreme care, hating every step, he climbed the pile of wood stacked beside the grill. *Pigs are not meant to climb,* he thought. *We hate climbing. Do pigs do tricks on balance beams? Do we ever ride bicycles? Of course not. All four hooves belong on the ground.*

At the top of the stacked wood, he poked his head into the grill. Ashes, hunks of old charcoal, bits of wood, all the normal stuff. He stuck his head in farther, until his snout smarted with pain. Underneath the stone chimney was something bulky.

Ernest inched forward until he got the thing in his teeth. It tasted of wood ashes, charcoal, and dirt. It smelled of smoke, the puppy, and milky formula.

I did it! he exulted. He raised his head joyfully, the blanket gripped in his teeth. As the logs gave way and tumbled to the ground, Ernest tumbled along with them. But he never let go of the red blanket.

When the logs stopped rolling, Ernest picked himself up, gave the small blanket a few good shakes, and headed for the house. He was tucking the blanket into the basket when Grampa came into the kitchen.

Grampa saw the blanket right away. "Look what our Ernest has found!"

Gabby flew in behind him, echoing, "'Look what our Ernest has found!'"

Ernest sat by the basket and felt proud. Grampa set the pup in its basket, and the tiny dog sniffed his blanket. He sat down, eyes staring ahead.

Jumping to his hooves, Ernest snouted the blanket into place around the puppy. "You just nap now," he told him. "This is your very own basket, you know. We're your family and this is your home."

"Ernest, you're the best pig that ever was!" Grampa said. "I wish I'd been there when you found that blanket. And see how much good it did for our little laddie. Look how bright his eyes are getting!"

Well, no, Ernest thought. *His eyes aren't bright at all, if you want the truth.* But he knew Grampa didn't want truth. Grampa wanted hope.

Gabby leaned over the table edge and gazed down at the puppy. She gave Ernest a doleful look and waggled her beak back and forth.

Grampa kept right on saying, "What a pig!" and thumping Ernest on the back. Ernest went right on feeling proud. Such a nice feeling.

After a bit Grampa said, "Now, if only we could find Milly."

10
The Search Goes On

AFTER LUNCH THAT DAY, Grampa spoke on the phone with AnnaLee. "We're okay," he assured her. "The puppy's eyes are open and—"

He grew quiet, listening. "Thank you. I'd love to keep him, of course, but he's taking just enough formula to hang on, and no more. It's called 'failure to thrive,' and after nine days, well . . ." Grampa's voice dwindled.

Failure to thrive? Ernest didn't like the sound of that.

From her curtain rod, Gabby looked down at the pup. "Wee laddie, wee laddie," she said, this time in a friendlier tone.

Ernest moved so that he sat next to Grampa, touching.

After a short conversation with AnnaLee, Grampa hung up the phone. When he left for the office, Gabby rode on his shoulder, but Ernest went to the aviary—known as Bender's Bird Camp.

"Hello there!" Ernest called, his snout against the wire enclosure.

"Hello there!" repeated a green parrot from a nearby crab apple.

Ernest said, "I hope you can help out. Grampa's having a bad time, and he needs to find someone. It's a cat—"

"And you came *here*?"

A yellow and turquoise parakeet fluttered to a branch below the parrot. "You're looking for

Grampa's cat, aren't you?"
she asked.

"Yes! Have you seen
her?"

"No, but please hurry up and find her!
Grampa keeps calling, 'Here, Milly! Here, kitty,
kitty!' It's making all our feathers fall out! The
white cockatiel, Lily, may never come out of her
house again."

"Oh, stuff it, Beverly," snapped the green
parrot. To Ernest he said, "We haven't seen the
cat, but if we do, I'll sing out. For Grampa's
sake."

Ernest thanked him and got to his hooves.
He heard the birds arguing as he went away and
feared he had just wasted his time.

Pastures next, he decided. *I'll do the llamas first,
and get them over with.* As soon as Ernest
squirmed under the pasture fence, the llama
leader galloped over. From his great height
Rufus glared down. "What are you doing here?
Where's Grampa?"

"Oh, he's working," Ernest said, trying to sound calm.

"You don't say." Rufus spat a stinking wad of green gunk just to the right of Ernest's head. Ernest backed up nervously. Llamas spit often, and for various reasons, yet he suspected they did it out of sheer cussedness. Of course, Rufus was not his favorite llama.

Do I even have a favorite llama? he wondered.

"Yo! Little pig," began Rufus.

"Excuse me!" Ernest said coldly. "I'm here because Grampa's cat, Milly, is missing, so he is very, very sad. I *know* you wouldn't want him to be sad. We need you to watch for Milly. Pass the word along if you see her, please."

The other llamas gave a few casual spits to one side and another. "We got the message," said one young llama. He zinged a revolting wad just past Ernest on the left.

That's it. I'm out of here, Ernest decided. He squeezed under the fence and called back over his shoulder. "Grampa will be very grateful!"

Ernest was more comfortable around cows. Even so, seeing them calmly grazing in the far pasture drove him wild.

"Don't just stand there and eat!" he cried. "This place is huge! We need you all to hunt for Milly!"

Lolita, Grampa's prize Jersey, shifted the grass in her mouth. "We heard she was missing. But listen to me, little pig. Eating is what cows do. We eat. We rest. We chew our cuds. We eat some more. Then we give milk. That's how it works."

"But this is an emergency! In an emergency, folks do what's needed!"

Lolita asked the other cows. Opal, Pearl, and Ruby all shook their heads. Lolita turned to Ernest. "That's it. Cows don't do emergencies."

Ernest made himself sound as pathetic as possible. "Not even for Grampa? For Grampa, who is *suffering*?"

"Oh. You didn't say that before." Lolita looked at the cows.

Opal said, "I'll take the south quarter and the long fence." She ambled off in a southerly direction.

Pearl said, "I'll do the north and that grove of trees."

Ruby said she would inspect the east side of the pasture and the creek that ran through it. Lolita promised to patrol the west. "I'll check ut those little bushes, and I'll tell Beauty to ep watch, too. She'll be happy to help."

"And you'll tell the goats?" Ernest suggested ·ly. "Grampa will be so very grateful."

* * *

Ernest was busy with chores the rest of the day, so that all he could do was worry. Night seemed extra long, but he used it for thinking.

Next morning, over in the office, he waited until Grampa left. Then he said to Gabby, "We have to make a phone call."

"The phone is put away now. In here." She rapped her beak on the offending drawer.

Ernest snouted the drawer open, and Gabby grabbed the receiver with one expert claw.

"Call Information," he told her. "Ask for the Animal Rescue League, and say that this is a emergency."

Happily, Gabby-Grampa did just that. ' please help me," she began, soundir Grampa, only very pitiful. "I'm Adam the famous veterinarian at the Bed ar my animal boarding facility in t' where every animal's needs are car

"Quit advertising!" Ernest said in a low, furious tone. "Describe Milly!"

"Yes . . . you see," Gabby-Grampa went on, "my beloved pussycat, Milly, is missing. She's just under a year old and has the cuddliest personality—"

"Tell them what she *looks like!*" squealed Ernest.

Gabby clacked her beak at Ernest, but complied. "Milly is the color of orange marmalade, with a striped tail. She has VERY SHARP white teeth—white tip on the tail—big green eyes—and a white bib under her chin. We all miss her and need you to look for her."

She gave Grampa's address and his phone number, and hung up.

Ernest closed the drawer on the telephone.

"I have to rest now," Gabby said. "All this is getting on my nerves."

Ernest headed for the house. In his mind he went over a mental checklist — chickens, animals in the pasture, birds in the aviary. *Everyone knows Milly is missing,* he thought. *So do the Animal Rescue people. I don't know what else to do.*

11

Ernest's Triumph

GABBY SANG OUT, "Hey there, Ernie!"

"Don't call me Ernie!" He drummed his hooves on the office floor and oinked his way around the room. Gabby sat still and shrieked at him.

Grampa came in the door, heard the commotion, and took over. With Gabby held against his chest, he sat down on the floor next to Ernest.

Patiently Grampa scratched Ernest's back and rubbed Gabby's head with his chin. "Okay, troops, I know everything's messed up. Our new baby is not doing well, and now Milly's gone. We're all in a muddle."

Ernest gave a soft "wrunk."

Gabby jerked her head up and down.

"I'm sure Milly ran off because of the puppy," Grampa said. "But life is always changing, you know." They sat for a long time, just being together. At last Grampa got up and went to his desk.

"I'll call the neighbors," he said. "I knew a tomcat once that moved next door. The pets over there got fresh table scraps, and at his old home they got dry kibble. He just moved to a better restaurant."

Ernest listened and thought, *Grampa sure knows cats.* And then something clicked. His brain gave him a truly outstanding idea.

Motioning Gabby to get on his head, he left the office.

Outside, Gabby fluttered excitedly. "You've got an idea!"

"Watch those claws! You ought to have a license for them!"

"Hogwash! Tell me your idea."

"They declaw cats, so why not birds?" Ernest cried, wincing.

"Bite your tongue! Are you going to tell me or not?"

By this time they had reached the barnyard. "Shh," Ernest whispered. "Don't make a sound!"

"*This* is your idea? *The barn? Haven't you already been here?*"

Ernest sat abruptly, tossing Gabby onto the dirt. "Yes, but not in the loft," he said. "We've been going at this all wrong. We've been hunting without thinking of *who* ran away. *Milly*, that's who. *So we have to think like a cat.*"

"I'll pretend I never heard that," Gabby said. She got busy rearranging her feathers.

"All right now. I'm Milly." Ernest thought out loud for Gabby's benefit. "And nobody loves me anymore. Just like when I was a kitten. Abandoned in the woods behind the barn. Mew, mew! I'm so frightened. I have to find a comforting place to hide. To be safe . . ."

Gabby squawked, "The hayloft!"

"Of course. Now shh!" Tiptoeing on delicate hooves, Ernest entered the barn and went to the foot of the ladder that led to the loft. "Go up there," he whispered.

Head cocked, Gabby said, "Are you sure?"

"Yes, because I'm thinking like a cat."

He watched as Gabby drifted upward on slow, silent wings. Having never been in a barn loft, he could only imagine what she would find, based on things Grampa had said.

He waited, hoping, and pictured it in his mind. Bales of straw and sweet-smelling hay. Tools seldom used leaning in the corners. Sun warmed the loft through the roof, and the animals' warmth came up from below. It was the coziest, most private place in the barn. *I'd nap there every afternoon if I were a cat,* he thought.

Gabby floated down as quietly as she had gone up. She perched next to Ernest on the barn floor, pointed her beak upward, and nodded.

Ernest leaped to his hooves. *Careful,* he told himself. *Say the wrong thing and she might run away for real. Someplace where we'll never find her.*

"Milly," he called. "*Please listen!* Gabby and I are here. We called the Animal Rescue League to find you." *And where the hay are they?* he wondered.

"Grampa called the neighbors," he went on. "We're all sad and worried. Remember how we felt when Grampa was sick? So please come back. Don't worry about the blanket. I found it, and it's fine. But Grampa *isn't*! Not at all."

Ernest stopped, afraid he had said too much, or the wrong things. Beside him Gabby waited, tailfeathers twitching.

A faint thump sounded overhead. In seconds, Milly's head appeared at the top of the ladder. "I didn't take it," she said.

Ernest blinked up at her. "You mean the blanket?"

"Right. You thought I took it, didn't you?"

He looked down, embarrassed.

"I knew it!" Disgusted, Milly sat and began grooming her left paw.

"Well, I was wrong and I apologize! Now come down and tell us what happened. Please!"

Milly finished grooming her paw first. Then, claws digging into the heavy sidepiece of the ladder, she descended to the barn floor.

"That's better!" Gabby said. "Now things can get back to normal!"

"It will never be the same again." Milly gazed dramatically off into the distance.

Ernest said, "That's okay! Life is more interesting this way."

"Don't lecture us!" Gabby squawked. "Anyway, we want to hear about the blanket. Milly, do you know who took it?"

"Of course. You see, after Ernest told me to use my head, I thought, *He is right. I love*

Grampa, and this is my home. But I did have to think about it awhile. The new baby's a dog, after all.

"But . . . I decided I could learn to live with him. So I came out from behind the stove, and the puppy was hung up on the edge of his basket. Trying to get out, I think. He's too tiny to run around, so I put him back in and took his little blanket outside to shake it. To make it fresh, the way Grampa does.

"I had planned to tuck him in, like Grampa," Milly went on. "I was going to tell him he was a stinky little orphan but that he could stay. As long as he behaved himself."

"And?" Ernest and Gabby said together.

"I was outside shaking the blanket and along came those crows."

"Those loudmouth crows from the woods?" Gabby asked.

"Yes. Three of them. They're huge! The biggest one grabbed that blanket right out of my mouth and flew off. I knew you'd all think I had

110

taken it, so I ran away. I was too scared to stay in the woods."

"I remembered that you liked the barn," Ernest replied. "That's why we came here."

"Stop bragging," said Gabby. "Let's go find Grampa."

On the way, Ernest told Milly how he had found the blanket.

"Oooh, those crows are so sneaky!" she hissed.

"Perhaps, but I am sneakier. My brain did it."

"You see why one pig per family is plenty," Gabby told Milly.

They found Grampa in the kitchen with a bowl
of tomato soup. He wasn't eating, just staring
down at it.

"Mewww," said Milly, going to sit by his feet.

"Milly! My marmalade kitty!" Grampa cried,
scooping her up. He held her against his heart.
"Ah, Milly, I missed you!"

She snuggled up under his chin and her purr
was loud.

After a time Grampa took all of his pets into
the family room. He sat on the brown corduroy
sofa, with Milly on his right and the puppy on
his left. He set Gabby on his shoulder.

To Ernest he said, "And you keep my feet
warm, you perfect pig. I know you found her.
You don't have to tell me." He gave Ernest a
slow, thorough scratching.

Grampa said, "Okay, troops, here we are, all
together—just like we should be. We need to

name our baby and get on with life." He looked down at the Scottie.

Ernest stood up so that he could inspect the tiny dog on the sofa. It was the first time he had really looked at him all day. *He's holding his head up,* Ernest realized. *And his nose is damp and shiny.*

Grampa talked to the puppy. "Somehow you've survived, laddie. You must have a good soul, so I'm going to name you after one of the noblest old Scotch souls — a famous writer — Sir Walter Scott."

KNOCK-KNOCK!

"Animal Rescue League!" someone yelled through the door. "You called about a missing cat?"

His eyes on the door, the puppy sat up and opened his mouth. At first nothing happened, but he kept trying. Finally he went "aarp" — a scratchy sound.

"Yarp!" he added a bit louder.

Grampa beamed. "My guard dog, Sir Walter the Scottie!" He got up and went to open the door.

"Hi there," he said to the man from Animal Rescue. "I don't know who phoned you, but my pig and my mynah bird found my cat. Thanks anyway for coming out. You folks do a great job."

The man in the green uniform looked pop-eyed at Grampa. "Your pig and your bird found your cat? Well, *sure*. Happens all the time. . . ." He shook his head in wonder and left.

"Yarp!" Sir Walter said again joyfully.

Ernest gave the Scottie a playful nudge with his snout. "See there, I told you it would work out."

Milly started in on the puppy's right ear. "It will take me two years to clean up this dog," she said.

Yes, ma'am, Ernest thought, *that's our Milly.* Satisfied, he flopped back down on the floor. His dependable brain had done it again.

To Sir Walter, Gabby said, "Welcome to the Bed and Biscuit!"

Author's Note

The animal behavior depicted in this book is based on well-researched animal facts. For instance, the hill mynah *(Gracula religiosa)* is the outstanding mimic of the bird world. Imported from Vietnam for eager American customers years ago, they are rarely brought here today, except for zoo display. They will eat almost anything but prefer fruit and live in tall trees in the wild. People who have owned mynahs say that they make superb pets but that they "have minds of their own."

Likewise the pig has a mind of its own. Of all domesticated animals, the pig is definitely the brightest, and probably the stubbornest and the sneakiest as well. (A few wild creatures — dolphins, whales, and chimps, for example, may be smarter, but you'll find pig proponents eager to debate this.) Given a chance, the pig will shower several times a day and never soil his living/sleeping area. A pet pig trains as quickly as a kitten, but the litter pan must remain in a consistent place. He's a stubborn critter, and he dislikes change. In France, pigs sniff out truffles. A trained pig can detect these underground delicacies fifteen to twenty feet away — and they're about a foot underground! Grampa is wise to let his mini-pig, Ernest, come and go as he wishes, for a pig hates being penned. As a born roamer, he lives to escape. As an infant, he is irresistible.

On to llamas. Yes, they spit often, and for unknown reasons much of the time. Like Ernest, I do not have a favorite llama.